I0654709

Laura Dayton Fessenden

Essie

A Romance in Rhyme

Laura Dayton Fessenden

Essie
A Romance in Rhyme

ISBN/EAN: 9783337054557

Printed in Europe, USA, Canada, Australia, Japan

Cover: Foto ©Andreas Hilbeck / pixelio.de

More available books at **www.hansebooks.com**

ESSIE

A ROMANCE IN RHYME

BY

LAURA DAYTON FESSENDEN

ILLUSTRATED BY J. H. VANDERPOEL

LEE AND SHEPARD PUBLISHERS
10 MILK STREET
BOSTON

ESSIE

PRELUDE

"It's a horrid bore," quoth my lady, "but I
 see nothing else to do.
They were very kind to Laurence," and here
 my lady drew
Her Point d'Alençon *mouchoir*, and wiped a tear
 or so
From her ruddy cheek (a tribute to her boy,
 dead long ago).
"Well, do as you like, my lady," says my lord
 from behind the *News*.
"Invitations I don't interfere with, so, my lady,
 do just as you choose."

THE INVITATION

MY DEAR MISS BRUCE. — We are nearing your
    annual holiday;

I presume it is rather stupid when your school-
    mates are away!

Do you think a trip to England your pleasure
    would enhance?

If yes, make your preparations for leaving *la
    belle France.*

I have in my home no daughters to help make
    time pass away

(Only Sir Charles and myself, dear), so I fear
    'twill be far from gay:

And McPherson (my son) is making, if I
    rightly understand.

An arrangement with a stag party to summer
    in Switzerland.

Another thing: we have decided not to open
    our house in town,
So I fear the attractions I offer are not of a
    kind to crown
A young girl's cup with pleasure. Still, dear,
    if you'd like to come,

And see the old house that Laurence told you
    of as "his home."
And see the mother that loved him (and misses
    him day by day),
You will find a kindly welcome.

                  From your friend,
                      MARY LANGLEY.

THE ACCEPTANCE

MY DEAR LADY LANGLEY. — I'm sitting in the
    horridest chatter and din

Of at least five nations of school-girls; so it's
    rather hard to begin.

To tell you how glad I am to leave this *la belle
    France.*

(If I'd been invited to Hades, last summer, I'd
    jumped at the chance.)

I had to show my guardian your letter that
    asked me to come

He's an American fossil, that used to live near
    us at home;

But, from being for years in Paris, he's grown
    to adopt their way

Of guarding wards and daughters, which, really,
    I must say,

To a girl of republican spirit, is just a regular
    cross;

For (to use a coined word of my country) each
    girl is about her own "boss"

In the land of the "Star-Spangled Banner," in
     that dear land of the free.

So I just *detest* Mr. Jenkins, and his *Frenching*
     it over me.

So when old Guardy Jenkins, in one eyeglass,
     tried to look wise,

And began a long string of questions, I felt
     my very hair rise.

And I said, "Look here, Mr. Jenkins, I'll just
     have you to know.

If you *shrug* and talk till you're *black in the
     face*, all the very same, *I shall go!*"

He gave in at once (per usual), he bade Madam
     "to prepare

Mademoiselle for a journey to England — Ma-
     demoiselle would summer there."

I am glad that you have no daughters, — girls
     always end with a row

Over some soft thing or other, one can't tell
     why, or how:

Then I'm glad your son's in the mountains, for
     I'm only just sixteen,

And men have a fashion of thinking a girl of
     that age rather "green:"

As for being out of a city, I've precious too
     much of *that* here;

And your proper London acquaintances would
  style me horrid and queer:
And then, my dear Lady Langley, it will be so
  sweet to know
I am treading the very pathways that Laurence
  trod long ago.

I was very fond of your Laurence: I liked his
  odd, foreign way:
And used to sit beside his bed in preference
  to play.

For you know, my Lady Langley, that Laurence was poor and ill:
And even now, in looking back, my eyes begin
  to fill.

From the first he seemed fond of Essie — Essie,
  my lady, is *me*.
I don't know how it happened — I was wild as
  I could be.

Mamma died when I was a baby, and so (though
  papa was refined)
I grew up wilful and slangy, and never was
  known to mind.

The doctor said 'twas consumption: that Laurence would have to go
Away from us, up to heaven, before the winter's
  snow.

Laurence was not sad at the summons: and
    once, when I was near
(I always was near him some way), he called
    to me, "Essie, dear!
Are your tasks for the day all finished?"
    "Yes," I said, "and what then?"

"Come and sit down beside me, and bring your
    paper and pen.
I want you to write me a letter: and, Essie,
    I want it to be
(Until I die), little Essie, a secret between you
    and me:

'Twill not be long, wee lassie (and I shall be
    glad to die).''

So I sobbed him out a promise, but he bade
    me " not to cry."

Well, I wrote the letter, my lady, how you
    read it, I can't think, I'm sure,

For I had no idea of spelling : punctuation I
    could not endure ;

But I wrote his words, my lady, and I'm sorry
    now to state,

That I just absolutely abhorred you, with the
    hatingest kind of hate.

What if poor dear Laurence had been wilful
    and wild,

It seemed so very unnatural that a mother
    should see her child

Turned in shame from the roof-tree, with a
    father's curse on his head,

Your husband seemed a monster : but Laurence
    always said, —

" Essie, I richly deserved it, I was wilful and
    bad :

I know my wayward spirit has made my lady's
    life sad."

You know how he asked " forgiveness "— that
    " kind memories you would keep

Of your youngest boy — your Laurence — who
    soon would be asleep."
So glad to rest in quiet, after life's short day,
But what's the use of recalling when I only
    want to say,
That I'm glad you forgave him, — glad that
    Laurence rests
With the turf of old England above him — the
    land he loved the best.
And as to our kindness, my lady, we Ameri-
    cans have a way
Of being a generous nation: of being apt to
    say
To a stranger that asks our protection, a "yea,"
    and not a "nay."
But enough of all this. I'll be with you ere
    the close of the week:
And, my lady, I really intend to be docile and
    gentle and meek.
I hope your son's in the mountains, or, if not,
    that we shall cry truce.
Believe me, my lady, I'm ever,

                    Your little friend,
                        ESSIE C. BRUCE.

ESSIE'S FIRST HOME LETTER

DEAR CHICKEN. — I've crossed the Channel, and reached the old English shore
(Every time I get on the ocean I'm sicker than ever before).
Old Guardy was true to the last; and stuck to me like a burr.
And the lectures and cautions he gave, will not in the least deter
Me from doing just as I like. Can a leopard change his spots?
"No, he can't." Well, do you suppose *his* talking would change me lots?
I said, why shouldn't "they stare;" I'm *very* pretty, grandpa,
You can't deny that; for they say, "I am like poor mamma;"
And that *she* was a belle in her youth, and *you* were her beau.
Till Dr. Bruce came and cut you out, so you can't be surprised, you know;

But in my heart. dear Charley. I felt a little
    bit queer.

A flutter of expectation. and a tiny bit of fear.

At the steamer's dock there met me. the stew-
    ard. a Mr. Ray.

He had come that morning from Leighcroft —
    all the way:

And his manner was so respectful that I began
    to see,

That if Guardy was provoking. he knew what
    ought to be.

So I vowed I'd be calm as a duchess. and
    that. all the way by train.

I would sit like a small stone image. and gaze
    out on the pelting rain.

But my legs got awfully cramped. (I had
    skipped my dull novel through).

And so I looked about me. as the next best
    thing to do.

Mr. Ray was respectfully napping. screened by
    the morning *Times :*

His snores were so funny and muffled. they
    made me think of the chimes

On our village church at home. Chick, I don't
    have need to tell

What I did. for you know I giggled — girls
    always do. and — well.

"I vowed I'd be calm as a duchess"

I could not very well help it, my eyes *would*
    take a look

At the others in our compartment, and there sat
    a man with a book.

I thought at first he was reading, but now I
    know that he,

With very much more interest, was calmly watch-
    ing me.

" *Ce monde est plein de fous,*" I've heard our
    madam say.

I wonder if that fellow, Chick, expected me
    to pay

Him back the laughing glances, such as he seemed
    inclined to bestow?

Chick, it *could* have been a flirtation (it was hard
    to let it go).

(But I did.) I gave back one vacant stare, then
    turned my head away.

And *kept it turned* (though my poor neck ached),
    till I heard the porter say,

" All off for Leighcroft Manor!" I saw through
    the door disappear

The heels of my would-be flirtation (I wonder
    if he lives here).

My dear, the carriage that met me was just a
    family ark.

And I really believe the servants expected a real,
    live, stark,

Staring, wild American Indian, with feathers,
    war-whoop, and all:

For, at sight of me their looks darkened, *I wasn't
    the thing at all:*

A miss in a Paris bonnet, en pannier, en high-
    heeled shoes,

Instead of a sooty savage in war-paint or with
    a papoose.

But servants are well trained in England, so
    they opened the old ark door.

O Chick, such *sniffy* cushions I never lounged
    in before!

Ray did not get in; he simply closed the door
    and stalked away.

And hastened to tell (I doubt not) the buxom
    Mistress Ray

And a host of red-cheeked daughters "that the
    importation had come:"

To call me a little "pipe-stem," and "thank
    heaven the girls at home

Had not putty faces and Chinese feet," and fifty
    other compliments,

That I won't take time to repeat. On we dashed
    through the twilight —

" Stood a gentle-looking lady. "

The village faded away — and there dawned upon
    my sight
The Manor: it stood upon a hillside, with ter-
    raced lawns before,
And, like some grand old picture, before the
    open door
Stood a gentle-looking lady, clad in soft robes
    of gray :
One glance in her face, and fears, Chick, fled
    on swift wings away.
By her side was a portly gentleman (he and
    Guardy would make a pair),
Very fat and comfortable-looking, without any
    stock of hair:
He hurried as fast as he could, and held out
    one puffy hand,
While he said in a *winey* whisper, "Welcome,
    dear, to England."
And then my lady caught me, and held me
    against her breast :
I looked at her through a mist, Chick, and felt
    more perfect rest
Than I have for two long years, since father's
    last kiss lay
On my trembling, trembling lips, on the day I
    sailed away.

It wasn't a bit like the stories (why will nov-
    elists lie?)

My lady was just a woman, and she let me have
    my cry

Out on her motherly bosom. Then she kissed
    me, and said, —

"There, there, you are tired, dearie: cease cry-
    ing, you'll make your eyes red."

Well, we had tea together, my lord, my lady,
    and I,

With no one but ourselves and a white-haired
    butler by.

Then we sat and talked of Laurence till the
    great clock struck nine,

When my lady said, "Are you ready for bed?"
    Be sure, dear, I did not decline.

Dear Charley, I'm awfully sleepy, but my room
    is very *swell*:

I wish it was not, I tell you, for it's rather
    frightful to dwell

With four huge life-sized pictures of some long
    gone ladies gay:

I can fancy them stepping down from their
    frames when the lights are taken away.

The bed is plump and fat and high, but yet I
    haven't a doubt

Every one of those four up yonder had on it
their " laying out."

But heavens! I'm getting the shivers, and I'll
frighten myself to death.

So, Chicken, I'm yours forever,

Your sister,

Essie, saith.

McPHERSON TO HIS FRIEND

DEAR PHILIP. — The fates were against me. I
     would not be able to say

What I said, and what I did not, when I knocked
     into our man, Ray,

And learned 'twas his charming mission to bring
     out *la petite squaw*

To summer at Leighcroft Manor. By thunder,
     Phil, what a bore!

I am sure my lord will endure tortures far worse
     than his gout ;

I thank heaven for Switzerland's journey, so that
     I am counted out.

But, as I said, luck was against me : for, I would
     have you know,

I had telegraphed my valet to send on word
     to Legrow

That I'd take the noon train for Leighcroft, and
     arrange with him then and there

For that sorrel colt — you know her? sired by
     " Young Golden Hair.

No time to lose, for Bronson was hard upon my
    track.

So I was booked and done for, and could not
    well turn back.

So I cornered Ray, and told him about my little
    fix.

Bade him not to heed me, nor let the little
    minx

Know I was son of my mother—no recognition
    to make:

But, by George! we got seats in the very same
    car. I donned my wide-awake,

And when the train got in motion, I took my
    novel out:

And, Phil, by all the powers! what do you
    think 'twas about?

I had bought the thing in London, at least I
    went to the stand

Near the depot, and took the book that lay near-
    est to my hand—

A little American story: the subject was very
    rum —

"Helen's Babies" I think the title—I tell you,
    I *laughed some*

Over the random purchase: but as 'twas all I
    had to read,

I found, in the little urchins, friends in a time
of need.

I wanted to get a look at my lady mother's guest;

But she sat with her face to the window, till
I thought I should not be blest.

When Ray dropped into a slumber, and sang
such a tuneful lay,

That the girl's face, from the window, turned
itself my way.

I don't think it's fair in a fellow to judge of
looks on a train.

Besides, *la petite Sauvage* had been out in a
pouring rain.

So all I can tell you is, that her eyes are large
and gray,

That her hair is brown, and was tumbled down
in a pretty sort of way;

But upon this atom of girlhood I did not waste
much time.

I was thinking of you, old fellow, and that soon
we'd begin to climb

In earnest the grand Swiss mountains; but, Phil,
I pause to say,

Can't you get off from town, if only for a day?

I want you to see my purchase; I came here
incognito;

But my lady has found me out, and so from
 the inn I go
To my old quarters at home. So come up, and
 bring some of the boys.
Sir Guinn if you like, or Tom, or our jolly
 friend Joe LeRoys.
And we'll talk our plans all over, and I will
 venture to say
There will be nothing stupid during your little
 stay.
Good-night, good-night, old fellow, now, is it
 not deuced queer,
That, after all my planning, I find myself just
 here?

       LEIGHCROFT MANOR.

I am more than sorry, my dear old Phil,
To hear by post that you were ill:
To know that you cannot, my dear old boy,
Take part with me in the wonderful joy
That Thursday evening holds in store. And I
 regret the forced delay
That still keeps back the wished-for day
Of our Switzerland journey. So haste and get
 well:
And, in the meantime, I've much to tell.
The fellows came up (five good and strong,

Guinn, Harry, LeRoys, Tom and Will Long).

They, thank fortune, were only a day behind
    me here.

So, you see, old fellow, I'd little to fear

From my lady mother's guest, who does not in
    the least advance

On acquaintance (she's a savage); and why they
    sent her to France

Is one of the unsolved problems. I don't see
    how ma has the face

To introduce *la belle Sauvage*: I think she's a
    perfect disgrace.

Her looks are all well enough, complexion, eyes,
    and hair:

In fact, I think she would be called by most men
    débonnaire.

But manners, Phil, she has none. I asked her,
    in casual way

(To open the conversation), how she came the
    other day?

I thought, perhaps, the pink cheeks might a trifle
    pinker grow,

At the seemingly innocent question: but, I would
    have you know,

She lifted her large eyes at me, and said, in
    a pert, brisk way, —

"*I,*' oh, *you* do not know, do you? I came by
 balloon from Calais!"

My lord led her out to dinner, she did not seem
 honored at all;

She talked with the ease of a duchess; informed
 us "of her skill at ball."

Said she " climbed trees, rode bare-back, played
 'shinny'" (great heavens! what's that?).

And another heathenish game called "cradle the
 cat."

The butler was highly amused; and so — strange
 to say — was my lord;

And my lady looked slightly perplexed, and *I*
 was horridly bored.

After dinner we walked in the garden. I plucked
 a rose from a tree,

And presented it to *la Sauvage,* saying, " *Oublier
 je ne puis;* "

And what do you think came her answer — " I
 would not if I were you.

But a man that makes a fool of himself is nothing uncommon or new."

And with this my gentle Savage took my prof-
 fered rose of peace.

While from *her* sweet society *I* quickly sought
 release.

The next day the boys came down: each I formally introduce.

To each, in return, a dainty *nod* vouchsafes Miss Essie Bruce.

I think she "takes" with the boys; she's inclined to snare

A fellow into thinking, late nights, of gray eyes and brown hair.

So Guinn has told me, Phil, and he's known as a hardened sinner.

Tom is growing fond of croquet, and LeRoys forgets his dinner,

In order to drink in the music of Miss Essie Bruce's voice.

(Miss Essie talks *too much* for me, but every man to his choice.)

She has won my mother completely.   Last night I happened to be

Out in the swinging hammock, the ladies were waiting for tea,

And I saw *la belle Sauvage* climb into my mother's chair,

And lay her head on her bosom (my lady's lips touched her hair).

And I heard her voice speak softly, saw her sweet eyes gentle grow.

Saw her red lips part in loving words (in words
    I could not know).

But the words brought tears to my lady's eyes,
    and brought kisses upon the face

Of the tiny creature in her arms (*for the time
    I'd have taken her place*).

Then Sir Charles calls her " his beauty," says,
    " when she goes away,

She will take all the sunshine with her for many
    a long, long day!"

The servants are her sworn allies: they laugh
    at her heathenish prank,

And still (*I* can't understand it), if Miss Essie
    held the rank,

In right, of a titled princess, they could show
    no more deference true

Than she seems to call forth from them when-
    ever her bidding they do.

But I'm off for a constitutional; and this even-
    ing, before I retire,

For your benefit, my invalid, I'll tune my feeble
    lyre.

No pun intended, old fellow (you know I'm
    renowned for the truth).

So, till evening, now I leave thee, O much loved
    friend of my youth!

ESSIE TO HER PAPA

MY DEAR, DEAR PAPA. — If you could only be
On this other side of the great wide sea,
That divides, with its waters of greenish blue,
Your own little Essie, your daughter, from you.
I know we'd be happy and merry and gay :
For, dear, dear papa, 'tis a glorious day —
A morning in June — not a cloud to be seen,
The garden is fragrant, the meadows are green,
And the river runs yonder — a silvery thread —
And the choir of robins just over my head
Are singing like "fury and all possessed"
To me (and three birds in a horse-hair nest).
Ah, if *ma tante* could be allowed from her
　　　grave to rise,
I think she'd change her will, when with opened
　　　eyes,
She saw how *much* of change had come o'er
　　　the orphan child :
What heaps of *savoir-vivre* had Mademoiselle
　　　Essie, the wild !

"My old maid Aunt."

"Speak well of the dead," they say: I wish I
    could now, *but I can't.*

For I always did, from the very first, detest my
    old maid aunt.

She called me "Esther" (through her nose), be-
    fore I hardly knew

The very difference between my little glove and
    shoe.

She always kept me "spick and span," she read
    me books on "infant sin."

And once she whipped me when I yawned and
    said, "O Aunty, that's too thin."

She punished me with Bible texts, and with the
    sweet commandments ten:

And, oh, in church, if I forgot one single small
    "Amen,"

A *word* in Litany or Creed, it was a sin of deep-
    est dye:

And if I did not mend my way, I'd rue it by
    and by.

She would not hear of fairy-tales — More and
    Edgeworth, goodey-good,

Formed my stock of literature — were my only
    mental food.

I'm glad our goat ate Hannah up: and I'll con-
    fess right now,

That Miss Edgeworth fell a victim to Bess —
    our brindle cow.

Well, she asked me one fine evening (I had
    been unusually bad),

"Esther, I'd like to know what you would do
    if you had

No kind aunty to love you, and to care for
    you day by day?"

I said, "I'll tell you, Aunty, I'd just be 'gailus'
    and gay:

I'd play with Chick and the fellows, shinny and
    marbles and ball —

I'd go without shoes and stockings, I'd hang up
    my French doll

On the topmost limb of the highest tree, and
    then I'd tell some lies,

And then (to know what it felt like) I'd set up
    a shop of mud pies."

That night she took a horrible cold, next morn-
    ing she made her will:

If I'd *cheesed* it about the lies (and the pies)
    she might be living still.

She left me all that she possessed — jewels,
    bonds, and land.

"To *me*, and mine forever," she said. But this
    was her dying command,

"That if her niece should live sweet fourteen
  to be,
She must make a journey across the great wide
  sea,
And enter a school in France; there must Essie
  remain
Three long and studious years, ere she journey
  home again."
And then she *gave us* old Guardy—"I do here
  provide
As guardian, Mr. Jenkins, a friend both true and
  tried."
Papa, two years of the three have actually flown
  away,
And there remaineth, father mine, but one little
  year to stay.
I left my native land, papa, a very rough, rough
  stone :
And I greatly fear, papa, Essie has not polished
  grown :
Still, I jabber French like a native, and I play
  six music books through,
And I know how to walk, to dance, and to talk,
  and there's the list, *Voilà tout.*
I'm afraid I have not forgotten old ways, which
  you will regret to see,

When I tell you I'm writing in pencil because
    I am up in a tree;

Yes, not a *little* tree either; but for comfort I'll
    hasten to say,

No one but the gardener knows it, the house-
    hold are all away.

My lady has gone with the vicar's wife to visit
    the village school;

Sir Charles has gone to a neighboring squire's;
    and the great big, stupid mule

They call their son McPherson (in a suit I'd
    blush to wear)

Is off with five boon companions pretending to
    hunt for *hare*.

I think I heard them say for *that*, but it may
    have been only *air*;

But whatever it is, thank goodness, he's gone,
    and where, I don't know or care.

Tell Chick my romance was *squelched*, that the
    wonderful *vis-à-vis*

Was no other than Mr. Mac Langley — how dared
    he flirt with me?

And then when we were presented, he asked
    me which way I came down?

I said, "By balloon, Mr. Langley." Pa, you
    should have seen him frown.

" Because I am up in a tree."

But McPherson is rather good-looking — he has
    dark brown eyes and hair;
But I know he likes fast horses, and I'm sure
    I heard him swear,
Under his breath, at his valet, for forgetting
    some trifling thing.
He's off for Switzerland next week; I'll be glad
    when he takes wing:
But, before he goes, my lady is going to enhance
My misery by giving me a little informal dance
On Thursday night on the lawn: "informal!"
    listen, my dear,
I want you to know the things they term in-
    formal here.
The invitations are written on *crested* paper, and
    say,
"It is Lady Langley's desire to make a pleasant
    day
For her young friend, Miss Essie Bruce: will
    the Misses *Blank* prepare
To meet Miss Bruce on Thursday next (if said
    Thursday shall prove fair)?"
The guests are bidden to croquet, the guests
    are asked to dine
With Miss Bruce and Lady Langley, if the
    weather shall prove fine.

Then my Lady Langley knows so well, young
    people do not scorn

A dance at any season, that she shall have on
    the lawn

A tent raised. There'll be music, and so the
    Misses Blank may

Prepare to wander through the dance and while
    the evening hours away.

I think I shall wear pink silk (I had it made
    on the sly —

Gave the order to Worth on a paper slip when
    Guardy turned his eye).

It's *snifty*, I tell you, pa, *princess*, train three
    yards long ;

Perhaps 'twill be rather *grand parure*, for I'm
    bound to get things wrong.

I suppose the guests will come, each clad in a
    book-muslin dress,

And behind their fans the dowagers will call
    my style "excess."

We will see — I'll write and tell you, oh,
    heavens ! what do I see?

McPherson and his friends, papa, are coming
    toward this tree.

McPHERSON'S LETTER CONTINUED

The evening is gone, and the night has been
    reigning for several hours.
Everything that I know of's asleep: from the
    garden the fragrance of flowers
Is stealing in upon me: 'tis a fitting time to tell
The rather strange adventure that to all of us
    befell.
Roys began it, I think: at all events, *la belle*
Was the theme we dwelt on. (I shudder as I
    tell).
Not for what *was said* so much as what might
    have been.
Phil, 'twill be a lesson, not soon forgot by us
    men.
At all events, Roys began it, said, " Take it all
    in all,
One would not call Essie *·ugly:'* for his part,
    he liked small
Women, like *la belle Sauvage;* then, as to her
    ways, ah, well,

She was very, very slangy! but, had she not
    to dwell,

All her young life, in a country of blasted
    plebeian breed?

For his part, he thought Essie did very well
    indeed."

Tom said, "The little foot that peeped out in
    croquet

Was really enough in itself to charm one's
    heart away."

Guinn said, " her eyes had a trick of looking
    one through and through,

Till a fellow caught himself blushing, as boys
    are apt to do."

But we all agreed her a *hoyden,* regretted that
    lips so red

Should so often give expression to words left
    better unsaid.

We agreed that our English ladies would vote
    her horrid and loud:

And then we asked each other, collectively in
    a crowd,

Would we be willing to offer ourselves to her
    for life?

Would any of us fellows be willing to take as wife

The object of our converse? "'Twould be being
    cut off with a shilling."

Said Guinn. "I could not ask her, even if I
    were willing."

Tom said they would be aghast: *his* relations,
    they'd raise a cry.

That made him say, at the thought, "He would
    not venture to try."

Roys looked glum: he said, "An officer of our
    day,

And particularly a junior, had plenty to do with
    his pay."

Well, we all said something, and probably would
    have said more,

Had not something worse than loudest cannon's
    roar

Reached our startled ears. A voice (not "gentle,
    soft, and low."

That excellent thing in woman the poet praises,
    you know)

Sounded high above our heads, a voice borne
    by the breeze,

A voice high up above us from among the
    garden trees.

Saying, "'Listeners never hear any good:' your
    comments have done no harm,

For in all your land, not a single man pos-
    sesses a single charm

For *la belle Sauvage*'! She *hates* John Bull.

Hates his arrogant, lordly way, and so accepts
this rather full

Dose of disapprobation. Does Sir Guinn fancy
his poky way

Of lifting his eyes,—a consummate art,—or
that polished flattery

Can win the heart of a girl American born—
of a girl who was reared to believe

That true manhood knows not how to deceive?

So, take the advice of Essie, each marry a flat-
footed girl.

Let each man fondly cherish as his, a native
pearl :

Wear her for aye on your bosoms and you will
never repine :

In conclusion, mind *your* business, and be sure
I will mind *mine*.

Now, if you'll kindly retire, I'll get down from
this tree :

For I've been up here all morning, and am
tired as I can be."

We left, Phil, without more ado, "*la belle*"
had us all in disgrace :

And we wonder how she will treat us when
next we meet face to face.

ESSIE TO HER BROTHER

DEAR CHICKEN. — The party is over. It was
 a most perfect success,
And I only wish I had the power to faith-
 fully express
The impression it made upon me. To give you
 a slight idea
Of how a social gathering is arranged and con-
 ducted here.
My lady bade me "be ready to receive the
 guests at four:"
So, just at five minutes of it, I knocked at
 her *boudoir* door.
You should have seen her stare, Chick! I
 know she thought I looked well:
But her English reserve and training would
 not let her tell.
I changed my mind on the pink silk that day,
 up in *the tree*,
And resolved to *out-do* England's daughters in
 primness, if *that* could be.

At the very bottom of my trunk (hidden away
    in disgrace,

From my puffed and furbelowed dresses) a
    white muslin had its place.

Simple as hands could make it. This I resolved
    to wear:

I knew that this sudden change would cause
    a general stare.

Well, on it went, this simple dress, with a rib-
    bon belt at the waist,

And at my neck and wrists I put a ruffle of
    soft lace.

My hair I did *la Marguerite,* and it hung
    like two coils of gold.

Ah, Chick, I knew I looked pretty, without
    even being told.

I took some half-blown rose-buds, and pinned
    them into my hair

("Marshal Niels" are very becoming to one
    whose complexion is fair).

And I did not put on a jewel, in ear, on finger,
    or breast:

Chick, in the code of simplicity I could have
    stood the test.

My slippers were only *thirteens,* as *la belle
Sauvage* has very small feet;

" Marshal Niel's are very becoming."

And a small foot on English soil, to an Eng-
    lishman's eyes, is a treat.

Well, we went into the drawing-room, and in
    very short time, my dear,

The guests that had been bidden — the guests
    from both far and near

Were with us. *We don't introduce*, that is not
    the *en règle* way.

The unknown guests of my hostess are my true
    friends for the day.

Every one talks to every one; but, were you to
    meet on the morrow,

A bow to these very same fellows would be to
    your cost and sorrow.

The five *Adonises* were on hand, *Sweet McPherson*
    at their head.

I never saw men look so foolish, or turn so
    lobster red.

As they do when we meet. I think that affair
    of the tree

Was about as jolly a thing as ever happened
    to me.

They feel so cheap, you know, to think I heard
    their talk.

Just fancy me falling a victim to a stupid
    English gawk!

And, above all, McPherson Langley! My dear,
    a bigger bore

Of a goose, and a silly donkey, I never saw
    before.

But I want to talk of the *party* — six girls,
    every one of them fair,

With the pinkest cheeks and the whitest teeth
    and the palest kind of brown hair.

Six fellows (five from our house), and to
    make the number right,

My lady had the kindness the young curate to
    invite.

We played croquet with a calmness that would
    make an angel fret.

I'm sure, "How could I stand it?" I just
    hated it, you bet.

I tossed the balls with a vengeance, I charged
    on the enemies' field,

Until *they* grew more earnest, and seemed less
    inclined to yield.

And then came the prosy dinner. McPherson
    escorted me;

And I made up my mind to bore him, to be
    slangy as I could be.

So I asked him by way of beginning, "if he
    had any money to spare?"

"If he had, would he *bet* I could not ride his
    colt, young 'Golden Hair'?"

He had a spoonful of soup raised at the time
    to his lips.

He tried not to look astonished, and took three
    tiny sips,

Then gave up and said gruffly, "Miss Bruce,
    you never must *dare*,

As you value your soul and body, to mount
    that colt, 'Golden Hair.'"

"Don't *dare* me," I answered bluntly, "or I'll
    ride her in spite of you;

For, if I'm told I must *not, that* thing I most
    surely will *do*."

He said, "Very well! as *I* pleased, but the colt
    was his, *he forbade:*

He should give *this command to his groom!*"
    and we were both of us mad.

And we never spoke another word. (McPherson
    glowered, I *planned*

How my Yankee wit could get of John Bull
    the upper hand.)

A heap of guests arrived at night, the lawn
    was a fairy hall,

With its tent and colored lanterns: of course *I*
    opened the ball.

You know what a ball is, Chick!—music and
dance, that is all —

Flirtation and whispered twaddle is about the
whole of a ball.

And we danced—the night wore on, and 'twas
very, very late

Before the last guest's carriage-wheels left the
manor gate.

Chick, *I have not gone to bed;* Chick, *I'm in my
riding-dress;*

Do you know what I'm going to do? I bet,
my brother, you guess.

Yes, he *dared* me not to ride; *he* to say to me,
" *I command!* "

I have no right to his old horse; but, Charley,
I won't stand

His saying what I shall do! Good-by! my last
words may be said:

Who knows but vicious "Golden Hair" may
bring home Essie, dead.

" Good-by! my last words may be said."

McPHERSON TO HIS FRIEND

DEAR PHIL, — Three weeks have passed since
    your letter came to hand,

And I'm sorry, dear old fellow, to have had to
    let it stand

So long, without seeming reason for such a long
    delay;

But when you hear my excuses, your wonder
    will pass away.

I meant to write you next morning — to write
    to you of all

That had occurred of interest the night before
    at the ball.

But what man so often proposes a higher power
    will change,

Disposing one's calculations in a way that seems
    most strange.

It was late ere the party was over; yet we fel-
    lows lingered still —

The smoke from our "*flor del fumas*" the de-
    serted tent did fill.

We laughed and talked of the ball, and some-
　　how when we came
To mention *la belle Sauvage*, we dwelt upon
　　her name
With a sort of tender accent: for, Phil, the
　　little sprite
Had (for some unknown reason) been charm-
　　ingly gentle that night:
Been gentle to all but *me*; and, like one that
　　is possessed
Of a devil, appeared Miss Essie, my lady mother's
　　guest.
She inspired a feeling of anger: and yet I'd a
　　sense of fear,
That this gray-eyed imp of girlhood was draw-
　　ing very near
Some dangerous experience. I led her out to
　　dine —
A penance, not a *pleasure*, yet, I could not well
　　decline.
I resolved to do the agreeable, *she* resolved the
　　other thing —
Result — all *my* good intentions in a moment's
　　time took wing.
Before the soup was over, Miss Bruce, with a
　　jockey air,

Bet me — mark you — *bet* me, she could ride
    young "Golden Hair."
I tried to keep down my horror, and (still more)
    my supreme *disgust,*
And that my replies were courteous I most
    sincerely trust.
I don't remember *what* I said, I only know it
    cast
An utter and perfect silence over our whole re-
    past.
Well, I thought of this all the evening, thought
    of it in the tent —
Thought of Miss Essie's flashing eyes, and won-
    dered if she meant
To defy my warnings; and I resolved to tell
    the groom
The earliest thing in the morning, that it would
    seal his doom
If ever he let a being, man or woman, young or
    fair,
Or ugly or old as Methuselah, mount upon
    "Golden Hair."
(So I said not a word to the boys, who had
    by degrees slipt away;
We were all in the land of slumber before the
    dawn of day.)

I woke with a start, the village bell was calling
    out for seven:

I turned upon my pillow, resolving to sleep till
    eleven,

When a thought of my purpose regarding young
    "Golden Hair,"

Changed my plan: I at once arose, and dressed
    me then and there:

I hurried down—the old house was wrapt in
    slumber yet,

And I laughed to myself, Phil, thinking, "for
    once I'll surely get

The best of *la belle Sauvage*: I'll stop this one
    mad prank,

Her neck shall not be broken, and she'll have
    me to thank."

The stable door stood open, the horses were
    champing their hay:

I called out for the groom, Thomas, he came
    with "Aye, sir, aye."

I gave my command at once: you should have
    seen the surprise

That came over the face of the fellow: you
    should have seen his eyes

Grow large with utter amazement. "Why,
    Master, you don't tell me so:

Miss Essie rid off on 'Golden Hair' more
    than an hour ago.
She came and bade me side-saddle the mare, she
    said ''twas a bet'
That you had made atween you: that she was
    afeared to set
On such a skittish young creetur as this 'ere
    'Golden Hair.'
I said all I could to dissuade her: but, Master,
    I did not dare
To say 'No' to such as Miss Essie: and, beside,
    I thought it your will.
I was *afeared*, I tell you, and am a fearing
    still."
There was no time for parley. I bade him saddle
    "Jane."
Asked which direction they took. "She went,
    sir, by hillside lane."
I wanted no more, but galloped away, my heart
    beating high with fear.
Dreading to look, dreading to think, of what
    might soon appear.
I galloped on: nothing in sight, all peaceful,
    calm, and fair,
No reckless Essie within view on more reckless
    "Golden Hair."

On I pressed, looked right and left, a curve in
    the road, a hill beyond;

At its foot, in the morning light, the waters of
    mill-brook pond

Glistened in the morning sun: then on my ear
    fell the din

Of the Eastern-bound train, to the town beyond
    coming in.

It turned a sharp curve on its way: on it
    came — God have mercy! — there,

With loosened rein, and laughing face, came
    Essie upon "Golden Hair,"

Riding along at leisurely pace: the memory of
    her young, sweet face,

As it looked in that moment of peril, Phil, has
    in my memory forever a place.

The beautiful, mettlesome little mare seemed
    pleased with the dainty burden she bore,

And turned her graceful neck to look at the
    face of her rider once more.

But the sharp, shrill whistle strikes on her ear,

Her nostrils quiver, her eyes grow wild, and
    her body trembles in nervous fear:

Another, another shrill resound, till far-away
    echoes take up the sound —

One maddening plunge, one wild rebound.

And, like the morning wind, on rushes "Golden
    Hair."

I looked in speechless terror, wondering does
    she bear

Her rider yet, or has she flung her precious
    burden fair.

No: bravely holding to the reins, on Essie
    came.

I strained my lungs, I called the name

Of horse and rider — "Whoa! whoa, 'Golden
    Hair'!"

"Keep tight hold, Essie, on that cursed mare!"

She heard my voice. I thought that I could
    trace

A look of courage on the pinched white face;

And back upon the breeze, Phil, this reply

Was wafted to my ears, "Give in to 'Golden
    Hair,' *not I!*"

And, sure enough, friend Phil, the mare began
    to slack,

And, as she drew up beside me, Essie remarked,
    "Mr. Mac,

I am *sorry* I took your dare, — a runaway is
    not gay, —

Mr. Langley, if you've no objection, I think I
    shall faint away."

I had her down from "Golden Hair" in less
    time than I can speak :

She lay in my arms like a lily, so gentle and
    white and meek :

Her brown hair all tossed and tumbled, her
    bonnet gone (Heaven knows where) :

But what woman wants a bonnet with such a
    wealth of hair?

I bathed her white face from the brook, holding
    her on my breast,

And I felt in this situation *particularly blessed;*

When the lovely gray eyes opened, and called
    me to earth again,

By the pretty lips remarking, "I think I'll ride
    home on 'Jane;'

I think I will, for my poor wrist aches like all
    possessed ;

And *you* can manage 'Golden Hair' a *little bit*
    the best."

Phil, since then she's been a lamb : and now
    that the boys are away,

I suppose I must give up Switzerland, and just
    resolve to stay,

And do the agreeable to Essie, — her vacation
    is almost passed. —

And try to make her stay with us pleasant to
    the last.

In three weeks from now she leaves us, and
    then I'm coming to town.

I shall feel quite like a hero, worthy of much
    renown,

For having made myself a martyr to be kind
    to this little child

(Who is not so bad, after all, Phil, only a trifle
    wild).

Well, my letter ends: I'll be with you as soon
    as Miss B. goes away,

And, for the present, Sir Philip, I wish you
    a very good day.

FROM ESSIE'S JOURNAL

WELL, little old Journal, my trusty friend,

Do you know my visit has come to an end?

And that I am back in the land I *adore* (?)

Monsieur "Johnny Crapaud's" dear, native
  shore!

My visit is over — my fair holiday,

With the things that *were*, shall be put away

Far in the past, that ever seems

To grow bright and more fair in memory's
  dreams.

When I came that day from *that* horrible ride,

I sort of and kind of *resolved* I'd decide

Never to take a *dare* again (I nearly broke my
  neck that day,

And, as a general practice, neck-breaking does
  not pay).

I resolved to utter fewer words in vulgar par-
  lance called "slang"

But, if life depended on keeping *that vow*, I'm
  afraid I'd have to *hang*.

Oh! when the whistle blew that day, and
    "Golden Hair" grew wild,

Every wicked thing I'd ever done since I was
    a little child,

Came before me *in a flash*, I thought my
    "bucket would kick,"

And I wondered if I was *so bad*, that his ma-
    jesty, "Old Nick,"

Would catch me from wild "Golden Hair,"
    and take me down to dwell

With Eurydice and himself, in his brimstone
    abode in — well,

I won't name the city — but I did not care
    to go :

I did not like the prospect, I tell you, "not
    for Joe!"

Then there came to me this comfort — I weren't
    so *very bad*,

And the Master, way up yonder, I remembered
    that *He* had

Known our sin and weakness, endured tempta-
    tion too;

So I was sure He'd open the gate and let *my*
    little soul through :

And in that sweet assurance my fears all
    slipped away,

While my heart asked God " to take me." and
my lips began to say —

"Now I lay me" —softly (as I do every
night).

But while I looked to Providence, you bet *I
held the reins tight!*

Then, lo! upon me dawned — now, Journal, who
do you guess?

Why, Mr. McPherson Langley, in his knicker-
bocker dress,

On his pretty mare called "Jane." with eager,
anxious speed.

He was hastening toward me. I was glad to
see him, indeed:

Somehow he was not so ugly, viewed by that
morning light.

And I don't think that *man* ever was so fair
to woman's sight.

Not Adonis unto Venus, not Æneas to the
queen

Called "Dido," with her wild love, looked more
beautiful, I ween.

He came from death to save me, ah! life is
very sweet —

We never know its value till death's dark form
we meet;

Till we see the arrow quiver, feel that the
    bended bow

Is eager to drink our heart's blood, and lay our
    head so low:

But I would not have him *know it* — know *I*
    was glad he'd come:

So I rode toward him madly, with lips both
    white and dumb,

Till I heard his voice ('twas music) cry, "Hold
    tight, Essie! Whoa, 'Golden Hair'!"

(He might have cried, " Whoa, Emma!" for
    all *that mare* would care.)

But "Hold tight, Essie," gave me courage, and
    I clung like all possessed,

While my heart beat, *oh! so* loudly, against
    my frightened breast :

But I answered, in my weakness, that *I* did
    not mean to let go!

And then ('twas a marvel) "Golden Hair"
    began to slow,

And grew slower, and still slower, in her eager
    pace,

Till Mr. Langley and Essie Bruce were actually
    face to face.

Of course, like a *fool* I fainted; I was mad,
    be sure of that :

So weak and *namby-pamby*, just like a regular
    "flat."

And when I sort of "came to" (but before I
    had strength to rise

From a very romantic position, and too weak
    to open my eyes).

I could swear, *if it wasn't wicked*, that I heard
    as plain as day,

McPherson say, "*precious* darling!" in the most
    smoodling way.

He call "*la belle Sauvage*" "*precious*" — call
    Essie Bruce "*darling*" too!

I wonder the earth did not open, and offer to
    let me through.

And then, — well, Journal, — McPherson, who
    looks with infinite scorn

Upon girls, and *green me* above all, *kissed me*,
    as sure as you're born!

I suppose I should have been angry: I'm a little
    afraid I *was not:*

An hour before I'd have slapped his face, and
    looked as angry and hot

As a large, new-boiled lobster: but there I
    lay, pale and calm

As a lily on a May morning, with my head
    on his great big arm.

But I had to come to myself: I opened my
    eyes and said, —

"O Mr. Mac, you're tired: I'm sorry my poor
    head

Proved so weak a member; thanks for your
    kindly support.

I won't faint *again*, I assure you: it's not *very*
    pleasant sport."

He said, "Thank Heaven it's over!" I replied,
    "Ah, yes, I survive:"

Then we never spoke another word for all the
    rest of the drive.

My lady never reproved me: and as for Sir
    Charles, he said,

"I was a trump:" he liked my pluck, so there
    was *nothing* to dread.

And then I spent three such weeks! McPher-
    son seemed to change:

And from that morning *I liked him:* and, what
    is still more strange,

He gave up Switzerland's journey, and devoted
    himself to *me*.

What caused all this sudden changing, I can't
    for the life of me see.

The days of the three weeks flew on great,
    wide wings away.

And before I knew it, Journal, had come the
    parting day.

I got up very early, intending to visit the gar-
    den below,

To say good-by to the landscape I had learned
    to love and know.

Then I passed through the rustic garden gate,
    to the meadow, where the dew

Lingered on the green blades and "violet eyes"
    so blue;

And I wished (a very silly wish) that every
    drop was a tear

Of regret, from Nature's children, that Essie
    was leaving here.

I stooped to gather some blossoms to take as
    mementos sweet

Of the pleasant visit ended, when the sound of
    coming feet

Rustled in the grass behind me, and lo, and
    behold! there stood

My stalwart friend McPherson, and he looked
    "very good"

(As the Bible hath it). His strong, blond Eng-
    lish face

Seemed full of feeling; and I'm sure that I
    could trace

A sadder tone in his full voice, as he said,
    "I'm glad you're here!"
"Yes? well, I came to say good-by to this
    meadow, grown so dear
To '*la belle Sauvage*,' your guest: I have spent
    such happy hours

Out here among the clover and the nodding
    blue-eyed flowers:
And I'm glad *you* are here: I can say good-by
    to you
In this meadow very much better than at the
    house I'll do.

Mr. McPherson Langley, if I've *ever* been hate-
    ful or rude

(And I can be *both*, I know, if it happens to
    suit my mood),

Won't you please forgive me? You know I'm
    a perfect child;

And I'm motherless, Mr. Langley, and I've
    grown up ever so wild.

When you first called me *la belle Sauvage,* I
    hated you with a will:

But now I ask as a *favor*, that *you* will think
    of me still

As *la petite squaw,* *la belle Sauvage,* as just
    wild little Essie Bruce.

With whom, after many a squabble, you've raised
    a perpetual truce.

And I hope and trust that some day we shall
    meet again :

And be assured, whenever it is, you'll find that
    you retain

My honest and true friendship: and I hope,
    sir, ere long to hear

That you've found the lady of your heart, some
    one just as near

Your idea of perfection as this earth can be-
    stow :

"I left a kiss on his forehead."

But it's breakfast time — by-by, for *please* — sir.
    I *must go.*"

He was bending over the rustic gate, his eyes
    looking into mine.

Mine that were brimming over with very salty
    brine

(Salty because I tasted one), and then — oh,
    Journal — don't tell,

For it's *awful* to act on *impulse,* but I *did,* and
    — and — well!

It was a motherly impulse, and he looked so
    very sad,

That I left a *kiss* on his forehead, and then
    took to my heels like "mad."

Journal, I never once looked back, I did not
    see Mac again :

For to my lady's amazement he took the noon-
    day train

To London: "important business called him at
    once to town."

Business! *his business!* I'll bet that nothing took
    him down

But to send on board the steamer *such* a basket
    of fruit and flowers

That I forgot to be seasick for actually several
    hours.

I'm back in the old dull routine, and I feel
    myself acting *queer;*

I go dreaming and *mooning* about in a way I'd
    have scorned last year:

Dreaming of great blond whiskers (that I used
    so much to despise),

Of an English voice, and, above them all, of a
    pair of dark brown eyes.

And I've actually *pressed* some flowers.   *Guardy*
    says, " I'm growing refined."

Perhaps I'm in (Heaven forbid it) — in love, or
    out of my mind.

McPHERSON TO HIS FRIEND

DEAR PHILIP. — I've no need to tell you of
    Sir Hugh's death last week :

The *Times* reported the sad event, so of that I
    won't stop to speak.

Well, we obedient relations, like a party of
    black crows

(Made me think of some scene from Dickens,
    in our sombre mourning clothes).

Followed the old man's body to its last resting-
    place :

And then I, seeing no reason to stay, turned
    my steps to retrace :

For I saw no need of my going back to hear
    the will

Of my maternal uncle, who never seemed to
    thrill

With an overflow of affection ; in fact, sad as
    it may be,

Sir Hugh and I had never been known on one
    point to agree.

When a boy I was always treading on some of
    his gouty ways.
And he did not seem to admire the course of
    my manhood days.
Then there were hosts of cousins who had hu-
    mored each caprice.
So why did I want to hear what he'd left each
    nephew and niece?
So I was rather astonished when my uncle's
    legal man
Begged "I'd return to the castle" with the rest
    of the mourning clan.
Indeed, he thought "I had *better*," so of course
    what else could I do?
And we gathered in the parlor, looking as cold
    and blue
As if from the bit of paper the lawyer held in
    his hand
We were to be perpetually blessed or irrevocably
    damned.
Ye gods! 'twas like a thunder-clap! Some
    legacies (very small)
Were left to others — to *me*, Phil. was given
    everything — all!
Titles, estates, rank, fortune, on this condition,
    my friend.

" *That I should marry a wife,*" Phil, "*before four
    weeks should end!*"

After the will had been read to my disappointed
    kin

(A will right and tight as a rivet). I tell you
    I felt *thin*

Over the stern proviso. Once I told my uncle
    that I

Had forsworn women forever, and a bachelor
    should die.

He never said pro or con, but hoarded it up in
    his head,

To make me eat with a relish my words after
    he was dead.

Only four weeks to choose a partner for my
    life —

Only four weeks to court a girl, and get her
    for a wife!

I could not keep the secret; and the girl I asked
    would know

That if she did not have me, I'd have to let
    all go,

And in the sweet by-and-by, when differences
    should be

Occasionally discussed between my chosen one
    and me.

She (after the manner of her sex) would not
    hesitate to tell

Me o'er again the story that I should know so
    well.

Tell me "I owed my title, my home, my wealth,
    my land,

To *her* wearing my ring on her finger, to *her*
    giving me her hand."

Then I thought over every woman known to
    me, high or low;

And to each "Shall I ask *her?*" my soul cried
    out loudly, "*No!*"

Did I say to *every* woman?   There was *one*,
    with soft brown hair,

And wonderful star-like eyes that kept coming
    before me there:

A little childish creature, with a saucy, *malicieux*
    face,

By Jove! Phil, there stood Essie! and *she* seemed
    to fill the place

Better than Lady Betty, better than Florence
    Bryne

Whose wealth is rumored fabulous (she's con-
    sidered a diamond mine

By fortune-hunting fellows), and she would
    give her hand

To one called Mr. Mac Langley, I've been
    given to understand.
But what's her wealth to the bright eyes of
    a little girl I know?
And what jewel does her casket hold that my
    darling can't bestow?
What pearl so fine and priceless as the per-
    fect teeth that show
Their whiteness in rare contrast to the red lips'
    ruby glow?
What diamond in the wide world can sparkle
    like the wit
Of the dashing little woman, when her lady-
    ship sees fit?
I could string her into a chain of jewels worth
    far more
Than ever mortal connoisseur had gazed upon
    before.
Ah! I, who had hated all women, was suddenly
    brought to see
That my only anguish now was, lest one
    woman cared not for me.
I resolved to make the venture; and *if* I did
    not succeed,
Why, I'd have to go in pell-mell and do the
    venturesome deed

Of blinding my eyes, and taking the first one
　　that came to hand :

So I gave my uncle's lawyer to thoroughly un-
　　derstand

That I *accepted* the arrangement, and, without
　　any further delay,

Would haste to ask the lady to speed the wed-
　　ding-day.

I stopped at Leighcroft Manor to tell my
　　parents the news :

To tell them of the bride I sought, and ask
　　them not to refuse

Their blessing if I won her. Imagine! 'twas
　　not a surprise.

My lady began to hug me, with tears in her
　　dear old eyes,

To tell me, "she hoped *it would be*, she had
　　learned to love Essie so,

And she did not think *her little girl* would say
　　to *her big boy*, 'No!'"

My lord had to wipe his glasses, said, "all *he*
　　had to say,

Was, when Little Sunshine came again, it would
　　be a happy day."

So I crossed the Channel, feeling *most* mighty
　　queer :

Feeling queerer and queerer, the nearer I drew
    near.

First I went to the guardian; he looked like
    one perplexed.

As if he very much wondered what was coming
    next.

He said, "to tell me the truth, *he* had very
    little to say

On this, or any matter, Miss Bruce *would have
    her own way:*

And that if *he*, her guardian, pronounced him-
    self content

With me, as Miss Bruce's lover, Dr. Bruce
    would give his consent."

So we went to the school together. Miss Bruce
    was summoned in;

I shall never forget the saucy nod, as though
    she cared not a *pin*

For her beloved guardian, still *far, far* less
    for *me*,

And had not quite decided *whom* we had come
    to see.

She nodded to her guardian, gave me her
    finger-tips,

But her pink cheeks grew pinker when I
    pressed them to my lips.

She snatched the white hand from me, saying,
   "Mr. Mac, do you know,

Kissing *saints'* fingers, *not sinners'*, is in Paris
   'all the go'?"

(Slangy little Essie!) I bent, lest Guardy
   should hear,

And whispered under my breath into her sea-
   shell ear,

"Kissing a sinner's forehead seems in *England*
   now the style,

So why should not sinners' fingers be kissed
   in France once in a while?"

Then Guardy found it convenient to take himself away:

And once alone, I hastened to say what I had
   to say.

I don't know how I did. When I thought I
   had it to do,

I pondered over the puzzle, wondering how in
   the deuce I'd get through.

But, by George! it was not so hard to say,
   "I love you, my dear!"

When the object of my affection was so very,
   very near:

Not hard to tell my story, when Essie's lovely
   eyes

Were looking kindly on me, in childish, pleased
    surprise.
She listened earnestly to me, a shadow on her
    sweet face
Of thought I had never seen before, adding
    new charm and grace.
Her head drooped low when I asked her "to
    be my own for life " —
Drooped lower still, when I called her "my
    precious little wife!"
Then I took her in my arms, and she raised
    her pretty head—
Phil, these were the very words that my be-
    trothed said, —
"I've got *plenty of money*, so I don't marry
    you for that:
And as for your *new title* I care no more than
    a cat!
But you've *got to* marry *some one*, I very plainly
    see :
And I suppose, take it all in all, you'd do as
    well with me
As you would with Lady Flora (or lady any-
    thing).
For *this* I know, your lordship, there is not *one*
    could bring

In her dower the gift *I* carry; and, Mac, I'll
    tell you true.

I've *tried all my might to hate you*, but I *love*
    you; *yes, I do!*

Mac, I'll try to be better; but *you* must be
    better still.

And if you are, old fellow, I think we can
    climb the hill

Of life very well together; and when we are
    old and gray,

We may be glad we promised to be man and
    wife to-day.

I am glad my lady loves me; and Sir Charles
    is a darling, dear,

And I'd hug them both, I tell you, if they were
    only here."

But I was a jealous lover; I wanted the "hugs"
    myself.

Phil, I think *I* shall be slangy, when I get the
    pretty elf

For a positive, life-long companion. We marry
    in two weeks' time.

So, come on, old fellow, and hear our wedding-
    bells chime.

Essie is blithe as a bird. I've promised the
    child, next fall

If the gods are propitions, we will go and make
    a call

On the land of the "Star Spangled Banner." I
    wish you could hear Essie tell,

The surprise she expects to create, it would
    pay your hearing well.

She says they'll expect to see her, majestic,
    stately, and wise :

And when they find only *Essie* has come back,
    their surprise

Will exceed anything ever written, for she never
    means to be

Anything but "*la belle Sauvage*" to the whole
    wide world and me.

I'm happy : yes, so happy, that earth seems to
    hold no cloud ;

I'm satisfied beyond measure, and very, very
    proud

Of my blithe and bonny darling : and, Phil, how
    in the deuce

Could I ever think "*Squaw*" or "*Sauvage*" in
    the least like ESSIE BRUCE?

FROM THE TIMES

At the Legation, on Tuesday last, were married,
    McPherson Langley,

Lord Crighton of Castle Wood, Thorn Hill, and
    River Way,

To Esther Carlton Bruce, only daughter of Dr.
    Gates

Bruce of New York City, in the United States

Of America.   The groom, Lord Crighton, stands

High as a scholarly gentleman, and ever warmest
    praise commands.

The bride, Miss Bruce, is beautiful, witty, accom-
    plished, refined;

Beloved by all who know her for both charms
    of heart and mind.

Owing to recent bereavement in the family of
    my lord,

And Miss Bruce being motherless, the wedding
    occurred abroad;

And was, we understand, a strictly private af-
    fair —

None but his lordship's parents and a friend or
    two being there.

We wish for my lord and lady all the blessings
    life can bestow:

May peace and joy be around them wherever
    their footsteps go.

www.ingramcontent.com/pod-product-compliance
Lightning Source LLC
Chambersburg PA
CBHW020041030726
47499CB00007B/2532